Maisley and the Big Day

Michelle Chan

Balboa Press books may be ordered through booksellers or by contacting:

Balboa Press
A Division of Hay House
1663 Liberty Drive
Bloomington, IN 47403
www.balboapress.com
844-682-1282

ISBN: 978-1-9822-5865-8 (sc)
978-1-9822-5866-5 (e)

Print information available on the last page.

Balboa Press rev. date: 11/12/2020

BALBOA.PRESS
A DIVISION OF HAY HOUSE

Dedication

Lovingly dedicated to my family; my wonderful parents, my beautiful husband and children, and my best friend who have always encouraged me and made this dream a reality. I love you all.

♥

Maisley was 5.

Being 5 was hard.

There were so many adults around her.

It seemed as though no one would listen to her.

She had something very important to say.

But her voice was so small.

Maisley tried to tell her mom but her mom couldn't hear her over her TV

It was too loud.

Maisley tried to tell her dad but he was at work and he couldn't hear her over the crackle of the old cb radio.

So, Maisley climbed and sat high up in her favorite peach tree, and tried to think, if only I were an adult.

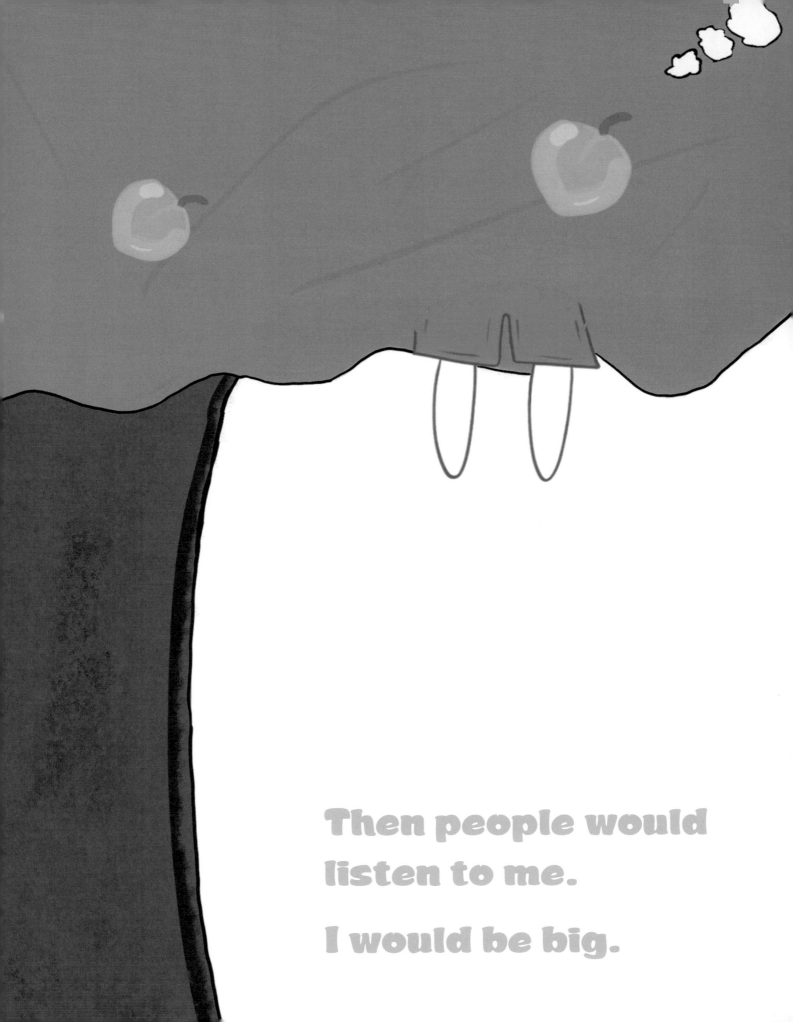

Then people would
listen to me.
I would be big.

Later, after supper, Maisley imagined what it would be like to be bigger. To walk around like a giant, and have heavy footsteps and a loud booming voice. Loud enough for everyone to hear.

But everywhere she walked she bumped into things and knocked things over. Being bigger was hard!

"Sorry!" she said.

"Oops!" she said.

"I'll clean that up!" She said, in her big adult voice.

She wanted to play.
She wanted to pretend.

But everything was
too small now.

Grandma saw Maisley bumping
into things. Grandma heard
her booming adult voice.

Maisley did not like
imagining she was big.

Being an adult was hard!
She was done pretending.

Then, Grandma came over to her with some warm yummy cookies and listened.

Grandma listened as she explained her very important thing. Her brother was mean.

She told her grandmother that he pulled her hair and did other very mean things and was not so nice.

So together, they walked to her brother and helped him to understand that

he used to give her
piggyback rides and
read to her every night.

Maisley sat and thought,
I think I like being small -
it's fine for now.

Grandma listens

being nice and loving to your family was much better than pulling hair and other mean things.

Grandma told them
about her brother and
how when she was little,

The End ♥

Acknowledgments:

A special acknowledgment to my Dad, for all of your encouragement and help. I would also like to acknowledge my son for his contribution to the creative illustrations. Thank you.

Printed in the United States
By Bookmasters

INSPIRATIONAL THOUGHTS

from the

Heart

— Volume One —

JACKIE AYALA MAGGIORE

Balboa Press books may be ordered through booksellers or by contacting:

Balboa Press
A Division of Hay House
1663 Liberty Drive
Bloomington, IN 47403
www.balboapress.com
844-682-1282

Cover and Book Design by Jackie Ayala Maggiore
Photographs by Jackie Ayala Maggiore

ISBN: 978-1-9822-5795-8 (hc)
ISBN: 978-1-9822-5545-9 (sc)
ISBN: 978-1-9822-5544-2 (e)

Library of Congress Control Number: 2020918316

Print information available on the last page.

Balboa Press rev. date: 02/03/2021

A Simple Loving Hug

A hug is an overflow of love
Covering and surrounding us
With warmth that grows
And begins to bring a sense
Of the meaning of love
Which is always at the core of our heart
Just waiting for that special time
To realize what love is
All thru a simple loving hug

Boys Town, Nebraska

Always Remember

Always remember you are truly and deeply loved

When you feel alone with no one to turn to

Always remember you are truly and deeply loved

When life isn't going as planned and you are out on a limb

Always remember you are truly and deeply loved

When you find that life has cheated you

Always remember you are truly and deeply loved

When you find that hopelessness and despair is upon you

Always remember you are truly and deeply loved

When you feel that love has eluded you

Always remember you are truly and deeply loved

Grotto of Redemption South Bend, Iowa

Amazing Things

Everyday people do amazing things
Of which we are not always aware of
Everyone has the ability to go beyond
Their so perceived limits and open
Their self-imposed limitations to
Move forward and make their dreams
Come to life and turn them into realities

Crazy Horse, South Dakota

Believe in Yourself

Keep your dreams alive
Don't let life's daily comings
Bring or keep you down
Start each day
With renewed anticipation
And lift yourself
Toward a new future
Believe in all
That you do
Only and only you
Can turn your dreams
Into a reality
By staying true
To your inner self

Devils Tower National Monument, Wyoming

Children

Children are our gift to us
Cherish your time together
Listen intently to their words
For they are speaking from the heart
Guide them to take time to marvel
In the wonderment of their surroundings
Show them through simple gestures
That they are deeply loved and
Instill in them that they are special
Acknowledge their dreams daily
And that it is possible to turn dreams into realities
Dance and rejoice life with them and
Always be available to heal their wounds
Show them how to stand and fight
For what is right for them
But most of all be accepting of who they are
And who they are to become

Petrified Forest National Park, Arizona

Dreams

Dreams are our yearnings
For what could have been
Reminders of what has been
And glimpses of what can be
Our dreams sustain us
And bring reason and meaning
To our daily existence

Crow Indian Reservation Plenty Coup, Montana

Enduring Moments

Moments are visions
Of past times
Spent with others
That endure and find
A place in our hearts
Where at any time
One can call upon them
To relive again and again

Napa, California

Friends

Friends are our someone
To confide in
To laugh with
To have wonderful nonsense talks
To have witty conversations
To call just to hear a voice or
Whenever we need to feel not so alone
Friends can be many things
But most of all they are the ones
Who make our existence meaningful
And stay along our side
Through our journey of life

Juneau, Alaska

How Lucky

How lucky to be given a life

To enjoy all the wonder and beauty

That surrounds us every second

In the timeless stillness that make up

Our being of here and now

So fortunate to be given this mere chance

To experience and absorb oneself

In the true existence of life itself

Venice, Italy

In Our Lifetimes

In our lifetimes we come across people

Who will surround and grab our hearts and souls

In a way that can't ever be erased

And as each day passes it is etched deeper

Within our being with an overwhelming

Persistence to be by our side

In our journey toward our own light

River Walk San Antonio, Texas

It Can Be Done

Time will no longer stand still
In idleness just waiting
For nothingness to hover over my existence
It's time to look deep into my lost dreams and
Pull them forward to wander and relive
The hope and desires I once had
But let slip away as I delved deeper in
The routines of daily life
It's time to move from this nothingness I feel
And open up my lost dreams
To feel to touch and wander in the
Hopefulness of what can still be accomplished
As I make the dreams I once had
Come alive and turn them into realities

Tracy Arm Fjord, Alaska

Journey

Look around
See the wonder
As it unfolds
Throughout the day
Blend into the realm
That begins to surround you
Absorb yourself in the moment
Reach for it taking it all in
Rejoice and become one
With your surroundings
As you go on your daily journey

Pompeys Pillar, Montana

Loss

If only you could feel my loss then maybe you would understand how my heart aches

And mourns for what could have been

My vision and hopes were shattered

The pieces no longer fitting

Will I ever be able to endure this loss

That is embedded so deep into the depths of my soul

Where it lingers and tears at the very essence of me

If only you could feel my loss

Then maybe you would understand

How my heart aches and mourns

For what could have been

Kern River, California

My Place

When I'm at rest my place calls to me

As I slowly dissipate into my place

I find myself connecting to a rhythm

That lures me to a pulse that surrounds me

And I'm willingly transformed

Into another level of time and space

As I join this steady and peaceful pulse

Becoming part of something

Much bigger than anything imaginable

My space over takes me and my awareness opens fully

As I settle into this realm where I'm reminded that

I'm a small part of a larger piece

And my space is there for me

Anytime I want to enter this new reality

Bryce Canyon, Utah

Open Letter

Today I sit and write this open letter

To say how much I truly miss you

Time stands still as memories linger

In my mind of the times we had together

Memories that are deeply buried in my soul

And burn brightly in my heart

Memories that bring back yesterdays of you and me

As my heart embraces these memories and reaches out

I'm once again surrounded by your presence

Allowing your thoughts and feelings

To merge with mine once again

Florence, Italy

Some People

Some people aren't given a chance
To lead a full life
They are put here to
Be our guide
To our life's path
And show us strength and love
Through their reason to be here
We are not aware that through them
We are being guided to a path
We are to endure during our lifetime

Mesa Verde, Colorado

The Independent Woman

The Independent Woman
Is confident as she moves and
Glides through the room
Touching everyone with her inner beauty
In small but precise doses
As they unwillingly become absorbed
In her presence

Savoca Sicily, Italy

Time

Now is the time only and forever mine
So much time has passed me by
Now here I am facing time
It's my time to reach and grab
What I've been yearning for
To embrace feel touch and marvel
In what time I can grasp and hold on to
As long as time will let me
I want to stop time for a moment and
Lose myself in its stillness
And absorb myself with the oneness of it

Minnehaha Park Minneapolis, Minnesota

Angriness

As we speak I hear the anger in your tone
I don't know why you are so displeased with me
Or what brought about this uncertainty about us
What lies beneath this unexplained anger
That you so easily toss my way to endure alone
The anger I hear from you is so disheartening and
Fills my inner being with sadness and hurt
If I knew then I could possibly put it to rest and
Clear the misunderstandings that linger about us
So lets put this unresolved anger to rest by coming
To a place where we can dispel any misconceptions
That started this mounting of such repressed anger
And be able to start a new day with a renewed sense
Of togetherness in a new place and time once again

Kern River, California

Courage

We never truly know the courage we have

Until we come across challenges in life

That grab a hold of us with such a force

And begins to surround us completely

We either go with it and grow in finding

Our essence of who we truly are or

We choose to wallow in our deficiencies

And do not discover the true meaning of courage

Forestiere Underground Gardens Fresco, California

Forever in my Arms

Forever I want you in my arms
Just to feel the pulse of your love
I want to hold you forever and
Let time stand still as we embrace
With no intention of releasing or
Breaking the connection of the oneness
We create when you are
Forever in my arms

Chapel of the Holy Cross Sedona, Arizona

Final Goodbyes

Today I said my final goodbyes to you
Even though I knew in my heart that
It was time to let you go my heart
Would not release you
Through the years you were always
By my side your presence always there
Just waiting patiently with love
Where I could reach for you
Whenever I needed comfort
So today for the last time
All my love and precious moments
Go with you as I say my final goodbyes

Yarmouth, Massachusetts

How do you forgive

How do you forgive

When the pain is buried so deep

And lingers with no place to go

Except to bury itself even deeper

Into your soul where it settles into its place until

Someone or something stirs it up again and the

Unbearable pain raises again to fill your

Heart and soul with an intensity that lingers once again

And you wonder why it doesn't get better

Joshua Tree, California

I Never Knew

I never knew you were leaving

So I didn't have a chance to say good-bye

To talk of the love we shared through the years

To reminisce about old times and share the laughter

And joy we once embraced throughout the days

If we only knew we could have been able to enjoy

The few moments we had left together

Since you have been gone I'm left with an open wound

So to ease the loss and pain within me

As each day passes I think of the times we had

I laugh cry and lose myself in the stillness

Of these moments and slowly as each day passes

I feel my loss and sadness turn to peace and

Acceptance as I relive the moments we once shared

Oatman, Arizona

Life

Life is the busyness
We spend every day
Doing what we do
To fill our spaces
And time while we are here
As the years begin to add up
And we get busily involved
In the daily livings of life
Time continues to pass by
Then one day before we realize it
We find ourselves older than we feel
And we're left wondering why
Time has left us so quickly
Putting us much closer to the
Limited time we have and now
More than ever we want to stop
Time and take each day to immerse ourselves
To live fully in the moments we still have

Flying into Pittsburgh

Longing

Time is still when I'm with you
As we connect and become
Locked in our time together
I cherish and immerse myself
In this wondrous space
That we create when we reach
Deep into our being to
Become part of each other
That feeling that I have been
Here before is one that I want to hold
With all my inner soul
As it settles into my inner self
And permeates completely all of me
With the belief that nothing
Can break this peaceful and safe haven
So I take this moment and splendor in its space
Until it slowly dissipates into nothingness
And I'm left longing for my next moment with you

Long Beach, California

Lost Dreams

Today I cried for all the times I've missed

I cried deep into my inner soul

That for each day I felt the hurt and pain

That was locked inside of me

It ached and hurt so bad

That all I could do was let my tears flow

But most of all I cried

For all the hopelessness

I endured through the years

Hoping that through this cleaning

That I will be able to start

A new day filled with hope

Kern River Valley, California

Missing Childhood Talks

We never talked as kids growing up
Our existence was be and let be
Do not speak unless spoken to
I missed growing up and
Not having the closeness of my siblings
That comes with the conversations of life
I missed the conversations of what could
Have transpired with our talks
I missed the closeness that could have been
I missed knowing who you really are
I missed knowing what your dreams were
I missed knowing your fears and challenges
I missed knowing what you were searching for
I missed being a friend when you needed one
But most of all I missed my childhood days
Of not being able to fully absorb myself
in your world where relationships grow
through the daily conversations of life

Mesa Verde, Colorado

My Five Stars

My five stars glitter brightly
In the sky twinkling peacefully
With an anticipation of insight that is
Waiting to be discovered

Pacific Ocean, West Coast

Right Now

Right now I want to feel and absorb myself in the wonder of life

Right now I want to love with all my inner soul and let my love melt into the path of others

Right now I want to see and become one with the beauty that surrounds me

Right now I want to absorb and linger in all known knowledge

Right now I want to enjoy other's company and dwell in their space and time

Right now I want to live open and free

Penn State Arboretum, Pennsylvania

Strength

I never knew I had the courage or strength

Until you came along

And showed me through your challenges

That all I had to do was reach deep into myself

And open the door of opportunity to take a chance

To reach even deeper and find courage and strength

Just waiting to be discovered that

I can truly be who I am

History Park San Jose, California

The Embrace

As I surround you with my embrace

The warmth of me and you

Slowly melt into one

And we find ourselves

Reaching and relishing the moment

As we connect to the oneness of us

Painted Desert, Arizona

Unknown to Us

We settle into a path that was
Put before us without thought or question
As our daily life begins to unfold before our eyes
And opens our existence we start to question our path
We seem to awaken from a deep sleep that protected us
And revisit our grounded beliefs that permeated
Every part of our being as we awaken
From this great sleep and the clouds clear
We for the first time see reality as our own
We tumble and fall and can't seem to grasp on
To something that is solid
Fear sets in and we know not where to go
Or how to function in this new reality
As we struggle we either embrace this new reality
With all our soul ready and longing for
A new beginning or we retreat back
Into our sheltered and small reality
Where all is not what it is but where it
Feels familiar in our comfortable safe haven

Penn State Arboretum, Pennsylvania

Uninvited

How did I get to this place
Where I feel so uninvited
Where I don't fit in
Where it is uncomfortable
And so detached from others
I long to get to a place
Where I am seen for who I am
To be able to grow and
Reach for the limit
A place where I feel at ease
And most of all invited

Bar Vitelli Savoca, Sicily

Words

Our perceptions and feelings are put into words

To help us express our thoughts to one another

We don't always use the right combination of words

That get us into situations we don't want to visit

But none the less we end up there

And find that we need to rethink our words

To get others to understand what it is we

Are trying to say

Kauai, Hawaii

Yesterday

Yesterday I learned
Today I explore and grow
Tomorrow I anticipate

Yellowstone, Montana

Dedication

This book is dedicated to my husband and children for their support and love throughout the years. I also dedicate this book to my grandchildren and all my future grandchildren.

Biography

Jackie has been writing since her twenties about life. She has kept her writings in journals because one day she knew she wanted them published. She is a freelance writer and photographer. On her journeys, she takes pictures that inspire her to write what she feels. She is currently retired and enjoys traveling with her husband throughout the United States and Overseas. She would love to hear your thoughts, you can drop her a line at: jackieayalamaggiore.com

Printed in the United States
By Bookmasters